The Strange Museum:
Pirate's Revenge

Strange Family Home

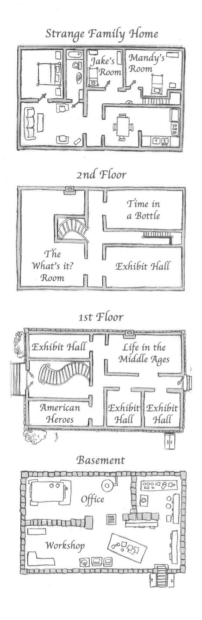

Jake's Room

Mandy's Room

2nd Floor

Time in a Bottle

The What's it? Room

Exhibit Hall

1st Floor

Exhibit Hall

Life in the Middle Ages

American Heroes

Exhibit Hall

Exhibit Hall

Basement

Office

Workshop

STRANGE MUSEUM

The Strange Museum

Pirate's Revenge

Written by
Jahnna N. Malcolm

Illustrated by
Sally Wern Comport

Gateway Learning Corporation
2900 S. Harbor Blvd., Suite 202
Santa Ana, CA 92704

ISBN 1-931020-09-4

First Edition
10 9 8 7 6 5 4 3 2 1

A short life, but a merry one!

—Calico Jack, pirate

Contents

Chapter One
Scared of the Dark

Mandy Strange was afraid of the
dark. She had always been afraid for as long as she
could remember. When she went to bed, Mandy
made sure she left her bedside lamp on. There
was a night-light in the hall. She had a night-light
in the bathroom. Her parents even left a light on
in the kitchen. That was in case she woke up and
needed a glass of water.

Being afraid of the dark was a secret. Mandy

had only told a few of her girlfriends at middle school about it. And she only told them when she was invited to sleep over.

Most of the time, it wasn't a problem. Except for today. Today, Mandy had made a big mistake and left her homework in the basement of her home. Her home just happened to be the Strange Museum of Lost and Found.

To make matters worse, her parents were gone. The basement was three floors down. And the lights on the staircase were out.

"Jake!" she called into her brother's room. "Where did you put the flashlight?"

"I didn't put it anywhere," Jake yelled back. "Why do you need it?"

"I left my history book in Dad's workshop in the basement." The workshop was where their father fixed all of the artifacts that came to the Strange Museum. "I have to study for my final exam tomorrow."

Jake opened his door. He was still in his jeans and T-shirt with the Strange Museum printed on the shirt pocket. It matched his sister's outfit. "Just flick on the light in the front lobby. That lights everything in the museum."

Mandy put her hands on her hips. "Before I get to the front lobby, I have to go down the stairs in the dark. Those lights are out."

"And my big sister is a 'fraidy-cat about the dark," Jake said in a baby voice.

Mandy made a face. "Like you're not! You know there's something very odd about this house."

Before it was a museum, their home had sat empty for years. People in their town said the house was haunted, and Mandy and Jake agreed with them. They had not seen any ghosts, but they had already had one very strange adventure that was out of this world. Just thinking about it

gave them both goose bumps.

"Take a flashlight," Jake said, stepping out of his room. "I think there is one in the kitchen."

Mandy shook her head. "I looked there and in the hall closet. It's gone." Mandy gave Jake one of her sad puppy dog looks. "Please come with me?"

"Nope!" Jake crossed his arms. "Remember last week? I asked you to help me with my short story for English and you said no."

"But I had homework," Mandy said. "Eighth grade has twice as much homework as sixth grade."

"Well, what about when I asked you to lock the museum so I could go to the movies?" Jake asked.

Mandy and Jake worked at the museum after school three times a week. Sometimes their parents asked them to be the ones to lock the doors when it closed.

Mandy rolled her eyes. "You were a jerk. I didn't feel like helping you that day."

Jake shrugged. "Well, I don't feel like helping you now."

"Be that way!" Mandy stamped her foot. "I'll go down those dark stairs and go through that creepy door into the basement all by myself." She waited for Jake to say something. He didn't, so she added, "If I don't come back, then you will be all alone. All alone up here at the top of this big old house. And, if something truly bad happens…," Mandy dropped her voice to a whisper, "there will be no one to hear you scream."

Jake felt the hair on his neck stand up. Why did she have to say things like that? His sister could scare him faster than anyone. Jake shut his book. "OK. I'll go with you this time. But then you have to do something for me."

"Like what?" Mandy asked as they left their apartment on the third floor of the museum. "I'll think of something," Jake said, heading for the stairs.

The staircase was carved from cherry wood. In the day it was beautiful. In the dark it was terrifying. It curved in a big *S* shape down to the next floor. Mandy waited for a cobweb to brush across her face or some slimy thing to grab her hand as they moved down the stairs.

When they reached the bottom of the stairs, Mandy put out her hand. She knew there were a few museum display cases in front of her. She didn't want to crash into them.

"Put your hand down," Jake ordered. "You might touch something. Remember what happened last time?"

How could Mandy forget? Last time their parents left them alone at night, their mom and dad had said what they always said: "Lock the doors to the museum, and whatever you do, don't touch anything!"

But Jake had ignored their warning. He touched a map in a glass display case. The next thing they knew, Jake and Mandy had gone back in time to 1775.

They met Paul Revere and rode a horse. They even went on Paul Revere's famous midnight ride. Mandy and Jake rode from town to town, warning the people that the British troops were coming. Almost as quickly, they had come back to their home in the Strange Museum.

Jake and Mandy had not really talked much about that trip back in time. There were days when Mandy felt it was all just some very strange dream. But Jake never forgot it. He often went to look at the silver coin Paul Revere had given him. It was now in a display case on the second floor.

Now, here they were, back in the Strange Museum of Lost and Found—after closing time.

Anything could happen!

Chapter Two
The Basement

"Boy, it really *is* dark down here,"
Jake said as they moved slowly
across the floor of the museum.

"No duh!" Mandy tried to sound
brave, but her voice cracked.

When they finally reached the basement door,
Jake found the light on the wall and flipped it up.
Flash! There was an explosion of light, and they
were in the dark again.

9

"Yikes!" Mandy cried. "Jake, why are all the lights going out? Is something the matter with the power?"

"Good question," Jake muttered. Goose bumps ran up and down his arms. "Um, Mandy? Do you *really* need that history book?" he asked. "Why don't you call in sick tomorrow? Then you can have one more day to study for the exam."

Mandy was thinking the exact same thing. Why go down into a dark, creepy basement if you don't have to?

"Come on." She pulled the sleeve of Jake's T-shirt. "Let's go back."

"Wait!" Jake said. "Do you see that?" A pale light glowed from under the basement door. "Dad must have left a light on in his workshop."

"Are you sure?" Mandy tried to remember if she'd seen that light before. Just a few moments ago it was pitch black.

"I guess that means you can get your history book," Jake said as he opened the basement door. They held hands as they walked down the steps. They stopped just outside their father's workshop. His door was open, and they could see what had made the glow.

A rusty lantern sat on newspapers in the middle of his worktable. There was a cloth next to it and a can of polish that their father used to make old things look new.

Their father's desk was next to the worktable. It was a total mess. Report papers and books were all over it. On top of the papers were some odd things. A stuffed bear with one eye leaned against a vase made with hundreds of buttons. A tin merry-go-round sat on a dictionary. Next to it was a very rare pair of eyeglass frames decorated in blue butterfly wings. On every shelf or tabletop sat a teacup. Most of the cups were almost full.

There was even a half-eaten sandwich on top of the phone.

"Boy, Dad is a major slob," Mandy said as she looked around the office.

"Where's your history book?" Jake asked, pulling a pair of socks out of an open file.

"I left it on his desk," Mandy said. "But now

it's over there by that old lantern. Dad must have moved it to his worktable."

"Well, grab it, and let's get out of here," Jake said. He still had goose bumps and the odd feeling that something strange was about to happen.

Mandy went to get her book. As she picked it up, she stopped to look at the lantern. It had eight sides with eight panes of glass. The top and bottom were made of tin, but there was no light bulb inside. A flame lit the oil lamp.

"Dad should have put this fire out," she said. "He could have burned the place down."

"Don't blow it out," Jake warned. "It's our only light."

Mandy smiled a wicked smile. "Who's scared of the dark now? Well, Mr. Scaredy Cat, I'll just take this lamp with us. Then we won't have to worry."

Her hand touched the tin lantern just as Jake

yelled, "Mandy! Remember the rule. Don't touch anything after the museum closes!"

Jake grabbed his sister's arm, but it was too late. The room had already begun to spin.

Chapter Three
On the Beach

Mandy felt a cold wind on her face. She could smell salt air. She had shut her eyes when she touched the lantern. Now she was afraid to open them.

"Jake!" Mandy whispered to her brother, who still held onto her arm. "Where are we?"

Jake was in shock. His eyes were wide open. He looked down at his feet. "White sand," he said.

15

He looked out. "Big blue sea." He looked up at the sky. "Sea gulls." He turned to Mandy. "We're at the beach."

"Beach!" Mandy's eyes popped open. "But what beach? And how did we get here?"

Jake pointed to the lantern Mandy held in her hand. "Well, you touched *that* even though I told you not to."

"Yes, but I touched lots of things in Dad's office and nothing happened."

"Those things belonged to Dad," Jake said. "This lantern is from the museum. It's one of the lost and found items. You touched it and now we've gone on another trip, just like the one we made to meet Paul Revere. Only this time I don't think we're going to see Mr. Revere. It's so warm, I think we've been sent to someplace like Florida."

"Why do you think it's Florida?" Mandy asked.

Jake scooped up a handful of sand. "This

sand is white, like the beach was when we went to Florida."

Mandy put one hand on her hip. "So maybe we're in California. They have beaches there, too, you know.

"It can't be California." Jake said as he looked behind him. A big sand dune rose up into the air. The sky above it was a soft pink color. "The sun is setting over there, and the sun always sets in the west."

Mandy squinted out at the water. "Then that must be the Atlantic Ocean."

Jake nodded. "I guess."

"This is just too weird," Mandy mumbled.

The two kids stumbled in a circle, trying to find something that would give them a clue about where they were. At the bottom of the dune were large gray rocks. Clumps of dry grass stuck out around them. A big clay bottle lay half covered by the sand. A tall wooden pole poked out of the wet sand. Bits of wood lay all over the beach.

"This beach is a mess," Jake said. He bent down to touch the pole. "It almost looks like a ship wrecked here."

"You mean, like a motorboat?" Mandy asked.

"No, a much older boat. Everything is made of wood and rope." Jake turned over a box. "This is a crate of some kind." He pointed to the tall pole. "See this? It could have been one of the masts."

"I think you're right," Mandy said. She held the lantern over a piece of torn white cloth. "I think this was the sail. And what's that?"

A silver button sparkled in the light. Mandy picked it up and read the words on it. "King George I."

"That's King George the First," Jake said. "When did he live?"

Mandy shrugged. "How should I know? That's

why I need my history book. I have to study."

Jake took the button from his sister. "This guy has got to be old. Look at his clothes. His hair is in a pony tail, and he's wearing one of those fancy coats."

Mandy put the button in her pocket. "Let's keep looking. Maybe we'll find more clues."

They were standing on a beach in a small cove. Only a few hundred feet out to sea were much bigger rocks. The waves crashed against them, shooting water high in the air. Jake spotted a starfish in a tide pool near the edge of the water. He knelt down to look at it and cried out in pain. "Ow! My knee!"

A round piece of brass stuck out of the sand. It looked like the bell on a trumpet. Jake brushed off the sand and tried to blow it. "I don't think this is a musical instrument," he said. As he spoke his voice boomed into the air.

Mandy took the trumpet from her brother. "I think this is some kind of speaking trumpet. Like a megaphone. You know, those things that cheerleaders carry." She held it to her lips. "We've got the spirit, so let's hear it! Goooooo, Wildcats!"

Jake took the speaking trumpet and pointed it at a small shack at the top of the dune. "Ahoy there! Anybody home?"

"That is none of your business," a voice said from behind him.

Jake and Mandy spun around.

Not three feet away was a girl about their age. She wore a long blue dress with a white apron tied at the waist. A cream-colored scarf was tied around her shoulders. A little white cap seemed to perch on the top of her wind-blown hair.

"Oh my gosh, it's Betsy Ross!" Jake whispered. "The flag maker."

Mandy, who was studying American history,

said, "That's not Betsy Ross. It's Martha Washington when she was a kid."

The girl stepped into the lamplight. She was barefoot, and her dress was old and torn. She held a broomstick in one hand and a knife in the other.

"I think we're both wrong," Jake whispered out of the corner of his mouth.

"Give me back my lantern," the girl warned, raising her knife, "or I'll gut you like a codfish!"

Chapter Four
Tess Reed

Jake stared at the knife in the girl's hand. It was long and sharp. He wasn't about to find out if she knew how to use it. "Give her the lantern," he whispered to Mandy between his teeth.

She shook her head. "No, Jake. The sun is setting. Then it will be extremely dark. You *know* how I feel about the dark."

Jake chuckled a little too loudly. "Ha-ha-ha. Well, I think you know how I feel about being gutted like a codfish on a beach in the middle of nowhere."

Mandy held up the lantern so she could see the girl's face. Her skin was tanned. She must have

spent a lot of time in the sun. Her wild blond hair was tangled and looked like she had not brushed it for days. She might have been a pretty girl, but her face was twisted into an angry expression.

"You boys give me that lamp, I tell you," the girl said again, "or I'll skin you like a possum."

"Boys!" Mandy put one hand on her hip. "I'm not a boy."

The girl was puzzled. She leaned in to look at Mandy more closely. "Then why do you dress like one? What navy are you with?"

"Navy!" Jake looked at his sister, then back at himself. Both were dressed in their jeans and blue T-shirts with the museum's name on the pocket. He could not deny that their clothes looked like uniforms of some kind. But not naval uniforms!

Mandy turned her head and showed the girl her dark ponytail. "I have long hair, see?"

The girl laughed. "So? I know lots of boys

with long hair. Why are you wearing breeches?"

Mandy was upset. How could this girl think she was a boy? "OK. Maybe I am wearing pants, but where I come from all girls wear pants." Mandy showed her the ring, gold chain, and locket she had been given for her birthday.

"Look at this. Do boys wear these?"

The girl's eyes grew wide. "Is that gold?"

"Yes, it is," Mandy said with pride.

"My brothers and I could live for a year on the money I could get for that," the girl said.

Mandy put her hand over the chain. "I'm sorry. But you can't have it. It was a birthday present from my mom and dad."

The girl flashed the knife again. "Then give me back my lantern."

"Who are you?" Mandy asked, taking a step back. "Why are you here?"

"I'll not share my name with you. And I

won't tell you what brings me to the cove on this moonless night." The girl's voice trembled as she spoke. "I'll just take my lantern and be on my way."

Now it was Jake's turn to be brave. "How do we know it's *your* lantern?"

"Because my father was a tinsmith." The girl pointed with her broomstick at the bottom of the lantern. "His mark is there on the bottom. T.R. for Tom Reed." She pointed to a small picture next to it. "And there is the date he made the lamp—1716, two years ago."

"1716!" Mandy gasped. "Then that makes this 1718."

She and Jake had traveled back in time almost three-hundred years!

"See that dent right there?" the girl went on. "Our mule Dolly gave the lamp a big kick one night when she was feeling mean. Of course, she feels pretty mean every night. But that's because she's hungry. Like the rest of us."

Mandy saw that the girl was very thin. She wished she had brought a candy bar or something to give her.

"If your father is Tom Reed, then would your name be Dolly Reed?" Jake asked.

"Are you deaf?" the girl shot back. "Dolly is the mule's name. My name is Tess."

"Tess?" Jake repeated.

The girl pointed her finger at Jake. "You are a clever one. You tricked me into telling you my name. That is not fair."

"Don't mind my brother," Mandy said. "He tricks everyone. He even told me that we were on a beach in Florida. But I said we couldn't be. Am I right?"

Tess blinked at the two of them. "I don't know what trick you are trying to play," she said, "but we are on the Outer Banks of North Carolina. That's Fishtown over there." She pointed to lights way off in the distance behind them. "And this channel of water is Topsail Inlet."

The wind had started to pick up. Thunder drummed loudly over the sea. Tess pulled her thin scarf around her body. "Now stop with the silly tricks," she ordered, her hazel eyes flashing with anger. "Give me that lantern before it's too late!"

The lantern was their only connection to the museum. It was also their only way home. Mandy was not about to give it up. Not when it was nearly dark. She swung the lamp out of Tess's reach. "No way."

Jake grabbed it from Mandy and swung it behind him.

The girl watched as the lantern rocked back and forth in the night air. "Careful of what you're doing!" she cried. "Do not swing it like that."

"Why not?" Jake gave it another swing or two, just to see what could happen.

The girl spun and pointed to the sea. "Do you not see that ship out there?"

Mandy spotted the outline of a big ship with three white sails. Lanterns glowed on its deck. "Where did that come from?"

"I'm not sure," Tess replied. "But if you keep waving my lamp, that ship will think it's a light in the cove. And it will sail to it."

"You're kidding," Mandy said.

"I would never joke about anything like that."

"So what happens if a boat sails to the light?" Jake asked.

The girl blinked at Jake. "Are you dim? It will crash on those rocks, of course." She pointed out toward the rocks just off shore. "And lives will be lost."

"What?" Jake gasped. He quickly dropped the

lamp to his side. "I didn't know that could happen."

Jake turned to his sister. As soon as his back was turned, Tess raised her knife above her head and ran at Jake.

"Jake, look out!" Mandy cried.

Jake spun around. For a minute Tess froze with her blade in the air. Then she did something that shocked them both. She sank to her knees on the sand and burst into tears.

Chapter Five

The Lost Boys

"Please don't cry!" Jake begged as he dropped to his knees in the sand next to Tess. "I hate it when girls cry."

"How am I going to get my brothers back, when I can't even get my lantern back?" the girl said between sobs.

"Your brothers?" Mandy sat on a rock near Tess. "Where are your brothers?"

"I don't know. I sent them to the beach to

find firewood today, and they never came back."

"Is that all?" Mandy waved one hand. "They probably rode their bikes into town. Or maybe they went over to the school playground."

The girl looked confused. "I do not understand. What is a bike? And a playground?"

"You don't know what a bike is?" Mandy gasped.

Jake tried to signal his sister. "Mandy, this is 1718. How many bikes and playgrounds have you seen in your history books?"

"Oh, right. I forgot." She turned to Tess. "I'm sorry. I was just thinking your brothers went off to play and forgot about the time."

"My brothers would never do that," Tess replied. "They know what danger there is out here. They know what happened to our father."

Hearing the word danger made Jake nervous. He looked over both shoulders. "Um, what happened to your father?"

"He was taken. A group of pirates grabbed him when he was gathering wood on this beach. I was up there at our house."

Tess pointed to the tiny white shack perched on top of a dune. It was at the far end of the beach and glowing in the last light of day.

"But why would pirates take him? Is he a pirate, too?" Jake asked.

"Of course not!" Tess's eyes flashed. "My father was a fine man. A good man. He took care of us after our mother died from a fever when little Will was born."

Mandy put her hand on Tess's arm. "I still don't get it. Why would pirates take your father?"

"Because they use men like my father as slaves."

"Slaves!" Jake's voice cracked.

Tess nodded. "On their ships. My father was fit. He was strong. He was perfect for them."

Jake spun in a circle looking for the bad men that made slaves of fit strong guys.

"So maybe he'll get away from those pirates and come back home." Mandy tried to sound hopeful.

Tess shook her head. "My father, rest his soul, is no longer with us." She wiped a tear from her cheek. "He was killed trying to escape. We heard about it from the man who owns the tavern in Fishtown. All the news passes through there."

"Oh, Tess," Mandy cried. "I'm so sorry for you."

"I am the head of the family now," Tess said. "I take care of my brothers."

"But you're just a kid," Jake said in surprise.

"I am nearly twelve," Tess said, holding her chin high. "I have been feeding my family for almost six months."

Mandy was two years older than Tess, but she

could not imagine having to be on her own and take care of herself and Jake. How would she get money? How would she feed them? She could only make hot dogs and popcorn in the microwave.

"What do you feed them?" Mandy asked.

"Not much." The girl looked at her with sad eyes. "We have had only cider and a little bit of hard tack for the last two days."

Jake had heard about hard tack. Sailors and soldiers always ate it. It was a stale roll that was rock hard and tasted like sand. No wonder Tess was so thin. In the lamplight, Jake could see the dark circles under her eyes.

"They must be very hungry," he said.

"Of course they are hungry!" Tess snapped. "That is why they went to the beach. To look for something we could trade for food."

"What would they find here?" Mandy held up the lamp to look around her. "It just looks like broken jars and old fish nets."

"Often times ships wreck against these rocks and their cargo floats to shore. There was a storm last night and the boys wanted to see if they could find any treasures." Tess's chin started to tremble. "And now they are lost."

Jake was feeling very jumpy. He picked up a rock from the beach and gripped it in his hand.

"Do you think these same pirates may have taken your brothers?"

Tess put her head in her hands. "It is my worst fear. I should never have let them come to the beach alone."

"But they are just children, right?" Mandy said. "Why would these pirates want children?"

"They use them as cabin boys on the ships. Like that one out there. They make them work as hard as the grown men. Like slaves," Tess said, with fresh tears coming down her cheeks. She put

her head back and cried, "Tim! Edward! Where are you?"

Jake and Mandy looked at each other. Then Mandy said, "Please, Tess, don't cry. We'll help you find your brothers."

Tess shook her head. "It is clear that you do not know this beach. You would do more harm than good. Now give me my light so I can go find my brothers alone."

Jake and Mandy didn't know what to do. If they gave the lamp to Tess, how would they ever get home?

The three of them stood frozen in place, looking at each other. They listened to the wind roar. They heard the thunder rumble off shore. Along with the thunder, they heard something else. Voices. Deep voices.

Tess turned to Mandy, her eyes wide with fear.

"What is it?" Mandy whispered as the voices

came over the top of the dune behind them.

"It's them!" Tess whispered back.

"Them who?" Mandy asked.

"Pirates!" Tess hissed.

"That's it," Jake said. "Time to go. Rub that lamp, and let's go home!"

Chapter Six
The Devil of the Seas

Five men stood at the top of the dune. All of them had beards. Each wore a long coat and shoes with buckles. Some had short pants, others long. One man had a red scarf tied around his head. Another pirate wore big gold rings in his ears. Each carried a lamp. But the one who was their leader was the most amazing pirate of all.

He stood in the middle, a pistol in each hand.

He had wild black hair and a long black beard that twisted into curls and was tied with black ribbons. The man was very big, almost a head taller than any of his men. His eyes were wide and staring. Two leather belts crossed his chest. Six pistols were stuffed in the belts.

"What have we here?" the pirate leader asked, pointing his pistols at the three of them. "A lass and two lads. And not a beard among 'em."

Mandy whispered to Tess, "Will you please tell him I am a girl?"

"I c-can't," Tess stammered. "Do you know who that is?"

"Captain Crunch?" Jake joked, half hoping he was right.

"Blackbeard!" Tess hissed.

"*The* Blackbeard?" Mandy gasped.

Tess gave a short nod. "The Devil of the Seas." Her face grew hard. "And the man who

killed my father!"

If Mandy's hair could have stood on end, it would have. This man, who looked like something out of a bad cartoon, was a real live murderer.

"Take them prisoner!" Blackbeard roared. "And be quick about it."

Three of the crew leaped down the dune. One went left and two went right. In an instant the kids were surrounded by pirates.

"Captain, we've no time to lose," the pirate with the scarf said, as Blackbeard came down the dune. "Our ship will be in the channel soon and needs our help to navigate—"

"Quiet, you fool!" Blackbeard roared. "Your lips are flapping like a sail in a gale." He looked back at the three kids huddled together in fear. "What nasty work brings you to this beach in the dead of night? Eh?"

None of them said a word. They were

too scared.

Blackbeard raised his pistols and moved toward them. "One of you had better speak, or these pistols will do the talking for you."

Jake started talking fast. "Um, we were just out for a walk, Mister, um, Blackbeard, sir."

"How do you know me name?" the pirate snapped.

Jake's mouth opened and closed, but no words came out.

Tess's face was white as a sheet as she said, "Everyone knows of you, sir, and your brave deeds. You have a ship called the *Queen Anne's Revenge* and a crew of three-hundred men."

Blackbeard looked pleased to hear about himself. "What else do they say?"

"That you're afraid of nothing," Tess added, "and that you like to drink your rum with gunpowder in it."

"Why?" Jake joked in a high, scared voice. "For a blast of flavor?"

Mandy shot Jake a dark look that meant *Shut up!*

"I hear tell that you have taken almost twenty ships as prizes," Tess went on.

"Twenty! That number is too few," the man with the earrings said. "Our captain has taken forty ships."

"Enough!" Blackbeard roared. His men fell silent. "I've heard enough." He turned on Mandy and Jake. "Here's what I think. I think you're Royal Navy spies, come ashore to find our hiding place."

"But that's not true!" Jake said. "We're just a couple of kids. Honest. We didn't mean to be here. We just want to go home."

"So why do you wear those uniforms?" Blackbeard waved his pistol at their jeans and

T-shirts. "Do you think I don't have eyes? These clothes are too fine for the likes of these island rats." He pointed at Tess. "See how her clothes are ragged and torn. Yet your outfits are new and have not a patch on 'em."

The storm was now raging. The wind sprayed sea water into their faces. A wave hit against the rocks with a tremendous boom.

The pirate with the scarf grabbed Mandy by the neck of her T-shirt. "I don't care if they're with the king's navy or no," he shouted over the pounding waves. "Let's feed them to the crabs now, before our ship comes in."

Mandy gulped. She could see Blackbeard was having second thoughts. It was time to act boldly. "Um, since you must know," she said in a loud voice, "I *am* in the Navy."

"The *Royal* Navy," Jake added. "And so am I."

"We work for King George," Mandy shouted

even more loudly.

"I knew it!" Blackbeard crowed. He turned to his men and said, "Didn't I tell you?"

Jake couldn't help adding, "And I'm a captain."

"You can't be a captain. You're too young," Mandy hissed at her brother. "I should be a captain."

Jake put his hands on his hips. "No! I want to be a captain. And you can be my cabin boy. Look, you owe me one."

"I owe you?" Mandy gasped. "For what?"

Jake put his face close to his sister's. "For going with you to the basement in the dark."

Mandy threw her hands in the air. "I can't believe you! We're about to be sliced and diced and you're fighting over who has the highest rank."

Tess shouted over Jake and Mandy, "The king has sent them to find two lost boys. They thought I might have taken them. But I told them

I know nothing about these boys."

At the mention of Tess's two lost brothers, Jake forgot about wanting to be captain. "That's the truth," he said. "We're looking for two boys. Two small boys who ran off from our ship." Jake leaned toward the pirate. "Have you seen them?"

"Maybe I have, and maybe I haven't," Blackbeard said with a sly smile. "What will you give me for them?"

Jake shoved a hand into his pocket. He found only a penny and two dimes. He looked at his sister. Mandy remembered the necklace and the ring. She hated to part with them. But she wanted to save those two boys.

"Here is a gold ring." She held up her finger and showed it to Blackbeard. "And I have a necklace that goes with it." She pulled the necklace out of her T-shirt so he could see it better.

Blackbeard leaned forward and smiled. His

teeth were black and broken. He smelled of rotten fish and gunpowder. Mandy wanted to hold her nose. But she didn't.

"I'll take that ring. And I'll take the necklace," he said in his gruff voice. He looked from Mandy to Jake and added, "And I'll take you three as well."

"What?" Mandy gasped. "But that's not fair!"

"Fair!" Blackbeard laughed as the pirates grabbed hold of Tess and Jake. "Who ever said a pirate was fair?"

As the pirates pushed Tess and Jake up the dune, the pirate with the scarf twisted Mandy's arm behind her back.

"Put 'em with the boys!" Blackbeard shouted. "We'll sell them all for slaves!"

Chapter Seven
Fight the Pirates!

As they came over the top of the dune, the three kids saw a campfire burning a few feet away. One big dark shape stood next to it. Two small shapes sat on a log nearby.

"Tim! Edward!" Tess cried out.

The two small shapes leaped to their feet and ran to their sister. "Tess! Tess!" they cried. "We knew you would find us!"

Mandy watched the boys run to hug their

sister. They seemed small for their age. Their shirts and pants hung like rags on their little bodies. Tess hugged her brothers tight and kissed the tops of their heads over and over.

The pirate with the scarf pushed Mandy and Jake forward. As he did, he called to the man by the fire. "Blackbeard says we are to put them on the ship when it comes in. Then they are all to be sold as slaves."

"That's what you think!" Jake cried as he jumped away from the pirates.

This surprised everyone. For one minute Jake froze, not knowing what to do. Then he remembered that he still had the megaphone. He put it to his lips and shouted the first thing that came into his head—a football cheer.

> *"Thunder, thunder, thunder-ation,*
> *We're King George's generation!*
> *When we fight with determination,*

We create a sensation!
Goooooo, Navy!"

Two pirates reached for their guns. "Where
are they? Where's the Navy?"

"They think you're calling the king's navy,"
Mandy hissed to Jake. "Keep it up."

Jake held up the megaphone again and shouted
into the dark. "We've got Blackbeard! And we've
found the boys! You can come out now!" Then he
added, "And bring the tanks and, um, planes."

Two pirates ran to the top of the dune,
holding their lanterns high. "Where are they?"
they shouted. "Can you see them?"

Mandy made a face at Jake. "Tanks? They
don't know about tanks or airplanes."

Jake shrugged. "Who cares. It worked, didn't
it? Look out! Here comes Blackbeard."

A single shot rang out and the crew fell
silent. Blackbeard held up his smoking pistol.

"Don't lose your heads, you sorry lumps of sea tar. Fan out, all of you. Check the beach and dunes to see from where this force may come."

The pirates split up and ran off into the dark. Their shouts flew back and forth on the raging wind. All you could see were the dots of light from their lamps, bouncing up and down along the beach.

"Here's our chance," Mandy whispered to Tess. "No one's watching us."

Tess looked around. Blackbeard had his back to them as he stared down the beach.

"You're right," she said. She took her brothers by the hands and yelled, "Run for it!"

The five of them raced for the water's edge just as a bolt of lightning burst above them.

Blackbeard's voice was louder than the thunder that followed. "Take one step more, and that step will be your last!"

Mandy and Jake shut their eyes and waited for the worst. Instead of a pistol shot, they heard the pirates cry, "Look out!"

Mandy looked up to see the shape of a black ship come out of the darkness right at them! Its white sails flapped and rolled in the wind.

"It's our lamps, you fools!" Blackbeard yelled. "They think we've told them to come in to shore."

"The *Revenge* will be torn to bits on those rocks," the pirate with the scarf yelled.

"Or on us!" Jake said.

"Run!" Tess cried. "Run for your very lives."

Chapter Eight
Safe at Last

Mandy did not dare to look behind her. She and Jake followed Tess and her brothers. They ran over the top of the dune and up a grassy hill. Behind them they heard shots ring out and the shouts of angry men. But there was a more terrible sound—the sound of the *Queen Anne's Revenge* hitting the rocks.

The air shook with one explosion after another as the ship's hull slammed into the rocky shore.

Above it all they heard Blackbeard yell, "Save my treasure, mates! There's riches fit for a king in coins and jewels on that ship."

Tess led them past a low shed and fenced pen. They could see Dolly the mule hiding from the storm in her stall. The house they had seen from the beach was very small. It had been painted white once, but the salt air had turned the wood a pale gray.

Tess opened the door and they rushed inside.

The oldest boy hugged his sister. "I'm so glad we're home. We were so afraid." The other boy pulled on his sister's dress and pointed at Mandy and Jake, who stood by the door.

"It's all right, Tim," Mandy said. "They mean us no harm. They can come in and warm their hands by the fire."

Mandy and Jake looked around the one-room house. It was bare but clean. It had a table and three chairs under one window. A bed stood in the corner. There was a thick bedroll by the fireplace. A big iron pot hung over the fire.

"These are my brothers, Edward and Tim," Tess said, her voice filled with tenderness.

The boys bowed shyly.

"And this is—" Tess stopped short. "I don't even know your names."

Mandy jumped in. "I'm Mandy," she said quickly. "And this is my brother Jake."

Jake waved his hand. "Hi, guys."

Tess pointed to the fireplace. "Come warm yourselves. Those pirates won't be looking for us now. They will have their hands full trying to save their ship."

Tim tugged on his sister's dress again. "Do you think the ship has any food or money, Tess?"

Tess put her arm around her little brother and said, "If they do, it is not for us, Tim.

Blackbeard and his men are on the beach.
They will make sure they save all they can from
their ship."

The boys threw their hands above their
heads and shouted, "Hooray! Blackbeard has
lost his ship!"

Mandy and Jake knew why the boys were

happy. They could not get the picture of the tall pirate with the wild hair and flashing black eyes out of their heads, and his nasty smile as he said, "We'll sell them all for slaves."

Neither could Tess. She sat both boys down on the bed and said in a grave voice, "Boys, we have no money. And once Blackbeard gets another ship, it will no longer be safe for us to live here."

"You mean, we have to leave our home?" Tim asked. "But we were born in this house." His lip began to quiver. "And Mother and Father lived here, too."

"And you could have died," Tess said. "The pirates would have taken you, and I never would have seen you again."

"That would be awful!" Tim cried. He put his arms tight around his sister.

Mandy felt her heart go out to the three kids. "I wish they could come home with us," she whispered to her brother.

"Me, too," Jake whispered back. "But right now I can't think how *we're* going to get home, let alone bring three more kids with us."

Mandy looked down at her hands. That worried her, too. How *would* they get back? As she stared at her hands, the fire sent a spark of light into the air. For an instant, the light made her gold ring shine bright.

"I've got it!" Mandy cried, leaping to her feet.

"You know how we're going to get home?" Jake asked. He was ready to go back. He'd had enough of pirates and shipwrecks.

"Not that." Mandy swatted at her brother's arm. "I know how we can help Tess and her brothers."

Mandy undid the clasp on her gold necklace. Then she slipped her ring off of her finger. "Tess," she said as she crossed the room, "how much did you say this ring and necklace would fetch?"

"A great deal, Miss," Tess replied, tilting her head to look at it. "Enough money to feed a big family for a year."

Mandy dropped the necklace and ring into the palm of Tess's hand. "Then you keep these. Find a new home. Feed the boys. And see what

you can do about bringing that pirate Blackbeard to justice."

Tess held out the ring and locket for her brothers to see. Then her eyes filled with tears as she said, "I cannot take this gift from you. It is too dear."

"Please, take it," Mandy said, trying not to cry herself. "It's worth far more here than where we come from."

"Bless you!" Tess wrapped her arms around Mandy. "What are you two? Angels that dropped from the sky?"

"No," Jake said. "We're just a couple of kids like you." He looked at Mandy and grinned. "Kids who were afraid of the dark and went looking for a lantern to light our way."

"And speaking of lanterns." Mandy picked up the lamp that had sent them back in time. "I think we can return this one to you."

Jake grabbed his sister by the elbow. "Uh, Mandy, are you sure about that? Remember, that lantern is what made this beach trip possible. I'd like to make sure this is a round trip!"

But Mandy had already given the lantern to Tess. The minute Tess touched it, there was a flash of light. Suddenly Tess and her brothers were covered in a thick fog.

"Good-bye, Tess!" Mandy called through the mist. "Good luck!"

As the mist thickened and rainbow colors swirled around them, Jake shouted, "We're going home! Hooray! There's no place like home!"

Chapter Nine
There's No Place like Home

When the fog cleared, Mandy and Jake realized they were standing in a dark room. During their trip back through time, Jake kept saying, "There's no place like home. There's no place like home." He kept on saying it even after the fog was gone.

Mandy jabbed him in the ribs. "Will you be quiet? We *are* home. I think."

Jake took a blind step forward and ran into

a table. He felt it with his hands. It was covered with papers, odd-shaped things, and a cup of water. "This is home, all right. I just stuck my hand in one of Dad's teacups. Yuck!"

Mandy waved her hands in front of her as she inched her way toward her father's desk. She found the desk lamp and flicked on the light. "It works!"

Jake was standing in the same spot he was in when Mandy had touched the lantern on the worktable. He blinked several times. "Whoa! What was *that* about?"

Mandy stared hard at her brother. "Did you and I just take a trip to 1718? And did we meet Blackbeard the pirate? And did we help a girl named Tess?"

Jake nodded. "Yes, yes, and yes. Don't ask me how or why, but that's what happened."

"Look!" Mandy pointed to her father's

worktable. "The lantern is gone."

"Of course it's gone," Jake said. "We gave it back it to Tess."

Mandy snapped her fingers. "And that's how we came home. She lost the lantern, and we returned it to her."

Jake nodded. "Our job was finished."

An old leather-bound book now sat in the center of the table, right where the lantern had been. "But look what's in its place," Mandy said.

Mandy and Jake moved slowly to the book. It was open to the first page. On one side there was a drawing of a pirate. "It's Blackbeard," Mandy whispered. "I'm sure of it."

"What does the writing say?" Jake whispered back. "Read it, but don't touch it!"

Mandy read it out loud. "Edward Teach was known as Blackbeard the pirate. He was called the Devil of the Seas by many that knew him, and I

was one of them. What I'm about to tell you is a true account of the sinking of the *Queen Anne's Revenge*, and of the final days of Blackbeard the pirate. Many think Blackbeard sank the ship on purpose, to steal his own booty. Blackbeard did indeed sink his own ship, but it was by accident. I know this because I was there."

"Look, Mandy!" Jake pointed to the name on the title page. "Look who wrote this book— Tess Reed."

Her name was printed under the title, *The Legend of Blackbeard*. In much smaller print was the date the book was published: 1730.

"Oh, Jake, do you know what this means?" Mandy whispered in excitement. "It means that my ring and necklace *did* make a difference. Tess was able to grow up and become an author."

Jake carefully examined the name under the picture. "I think Tess isn't the only one who did well. I believe the name under this drawing is Tim Reed, her baby brother."

"Let's check the cover to see if their names are there." Mandy put out her hand to pick up the book.

"Careful!" Jake caught hold of her arm. "If you touch that book we may find ourselves on another trip. I want to stay home now."

"I think this book is a thank-you to us for returning the lamp," Mandy said. "Just like the coin was a gift from Paul Revere when we went on our first trip back in time."

"I hope you're right." Jake shut his eyes and held his breath as Mandy closed the book cover and picked it up.

Nothing happened.

Jake let out a gush of air. "Good! Now let's get out of here before we touch some other museum piece that really *will* take us somewhere we don't want to go!"

"Good idea." Mandy remembered that she still needed to study for her exam. She picked up her history book. But so much had happened that night, it was hard to imagine being able to put any other thoughts into her head.

Jake crossed to his father's desk lamp. "Do you want me to leave this on?" he asked his sister.

"No," Mandy said bravely. "You can turn it off."

"It's going to be very dark in the lobby," Jake warned. "Remember, something's wrong with the electricity."

"Still?" Mandy asked.

"Of course." Jake tapped his watch. "We've only been gone a minute or two. That's hardly enough time for the power company to come and fix the lights."

"Oh," Mandy chuckled. "I forgot."

Jake reached for the desk lamp again. "Are you sure you won't be scared?"

Mandy thought about it for a moment. "No. I think I just discovered that there are a lot of things more scary than the dark."

"Like pirates?" Jake said, remembering Blackbeard's wild black eyes and the pistols he pointed straight at them.

"Like not knowing where your next meal will come from. Or how you will be able to feed your family." Mandy thought of Tess and her two young brothers. She turned off her father's desk lamp, took Jake's hand, and led them to the basement stairs.

Just as they were about to climb up, Jake stopped cold.

"What's the matter?" Mandy asked. "Let's hurry up and get upstairs."

Jake gulped. "Um, I was just thinking about

that creep, Blackbeard. Wasn't he supposed to have some kind of ghost?"

"Ghost?" Mandy froze with one foot in the air.

"Yeah, ghost."

Mandy did an about-face. "On second thought," she said, "why don't we just stay here in Dad's office? He and Mom should be home soon. He's got a light, lots of cold tea, and, well, I can study down here."

Jake breathed a sigh of relief. "That's the best idea you've had all night!"

About the Authors

JAHNNA N. MALCOLM stands for Jahnna "and" Malcolm. Jahnna Beecham and Malcolm Hillgartner are married and have published over ninety books for kids and teens. They've written about ballerinas, horses, ghosts, singing cowboys, and green slime. Their most recent book series is called The Jewel Kingdom, and it is about adventurous princesses. They even made a movie of the first book in the series, *The Ruby Princess Runs Away*.

Before Jahnna and Malcolm wrote books, they were actors. They met on the stage and were married on the stage, and now they live in Oregon. They used to think of their ideas for their books by themselves. Now they get help from their son, Dash, and daughter, Skye.

About the Illustrator

SALLY WERN CONMPORT'S illustrations have been seen nationally for over fifteen years. A 1976 graduate of Columbus College of Art & Design, she began her career as an art director at several agencies before beginning full-time illustration in 1983. Her work has received numerous honors including The Society of Illustrators, Communication Arts, *Print* magazine, *How* magazine, and many Addy awards.

Sally's artwork has been included in several permanent collections, including Women Illustrators from the permanent collection of The Society of Illustrators. Her first children's book, *Brave Margaret*, was released in February 1999. Sally lives with her husband and two children in Annapolis, Maryland.